CAPTAIN BOB
Sets Sail

BY **Roni Schotter**

ILLUSTRATED BY **Joe Cepeda**

An Anne Schwartz Book

Atheneum Books *for* Young Readers

He was Captain Bob,
and he was the bravest
and best captain that ever sailed
the Soapy Seas.

With his sea scarf around his neck and spyglass in hand, he stepped into the warm waters of Bath Bay. "Heave ho, ready to go!" he shouted, and was off.

It was a crowded bay. There were ducks and
deep-diving dinosaurs and boats bobbing and
banging and splashing and crashing. It was
a soap-sinking sea, but Bob only laughed—
"Ha ha!"—for he was Captain.

The sea was rising high, and it was Bob's job to stop it. "Hip! Ship! Ahoy!" he cried, and paddled fast toward Faucet Falls.

But then, danger!
He was attacked from behind
by a ruby-ringed Sea Hand.

Wiggle he might, there was *no* escape.
The Sea Hand held him steady in her grip.
But Bob wasn't afraid. He tossed back his
head and called out, "Wash me! Slosh me!
You'll never ever squash me!"

At last Bob floated free, into the surging, sudsy sea.
He dipped his chin in, beat his belly, and bellowed,
"I'm Captain Bob, the Mighty Soap Beard.
To Faucet Falls. Away!"

Then, with a swish like a fish, he swam across Bath Bay.

Faucet Falls rumbled and poured and tumbled down in a terrible rush, but Bob bravely shouted, **"Hush!"** And, with a roar, he turned the knobs and the water was no more.

His job well done,
   he laughed,
      "Ho ho hum!"
         It was time for
            a scrub down,
               a rub-a-dubba-dub down.

And finally, a float, tummy up, dreaming
of splendid creatures of the deep.

But the waters of Bath Bay were cold now—
bone chilling.
"Sh-sh-sh-shake and
sh-shiver and quiver me timbers,"
Bob chattered.
"It's t-t-time to go.
Attention all ships.
Land ho!"

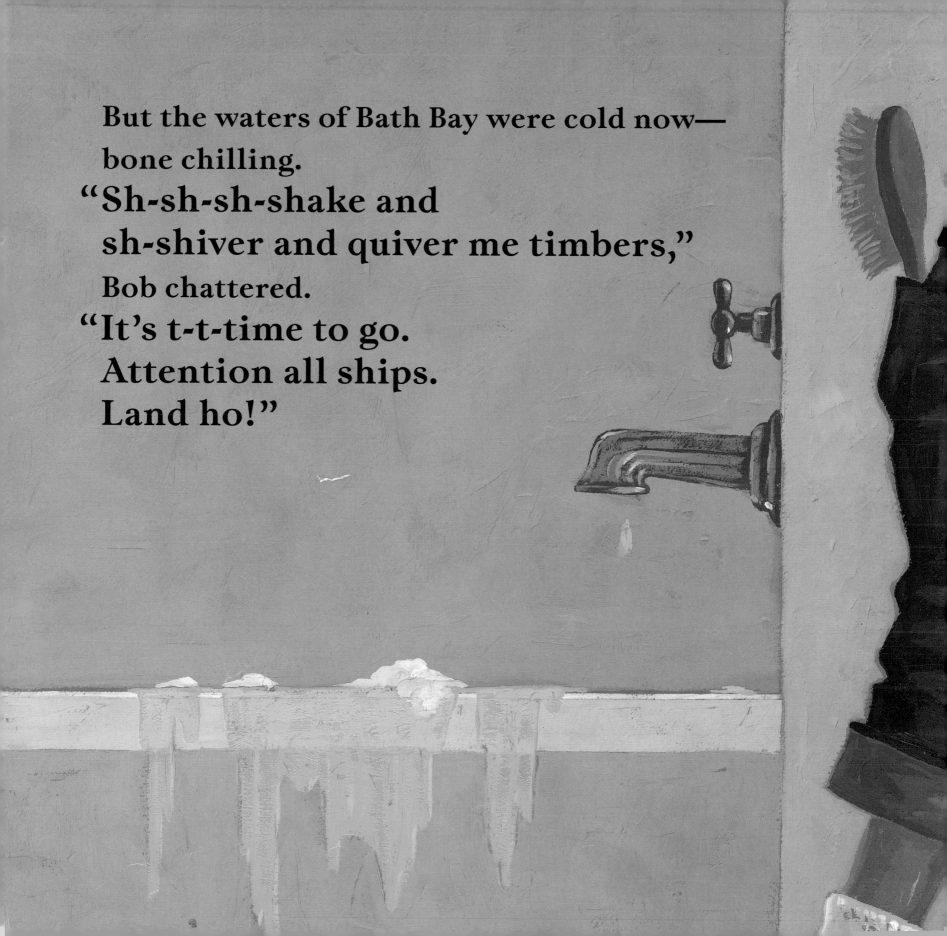

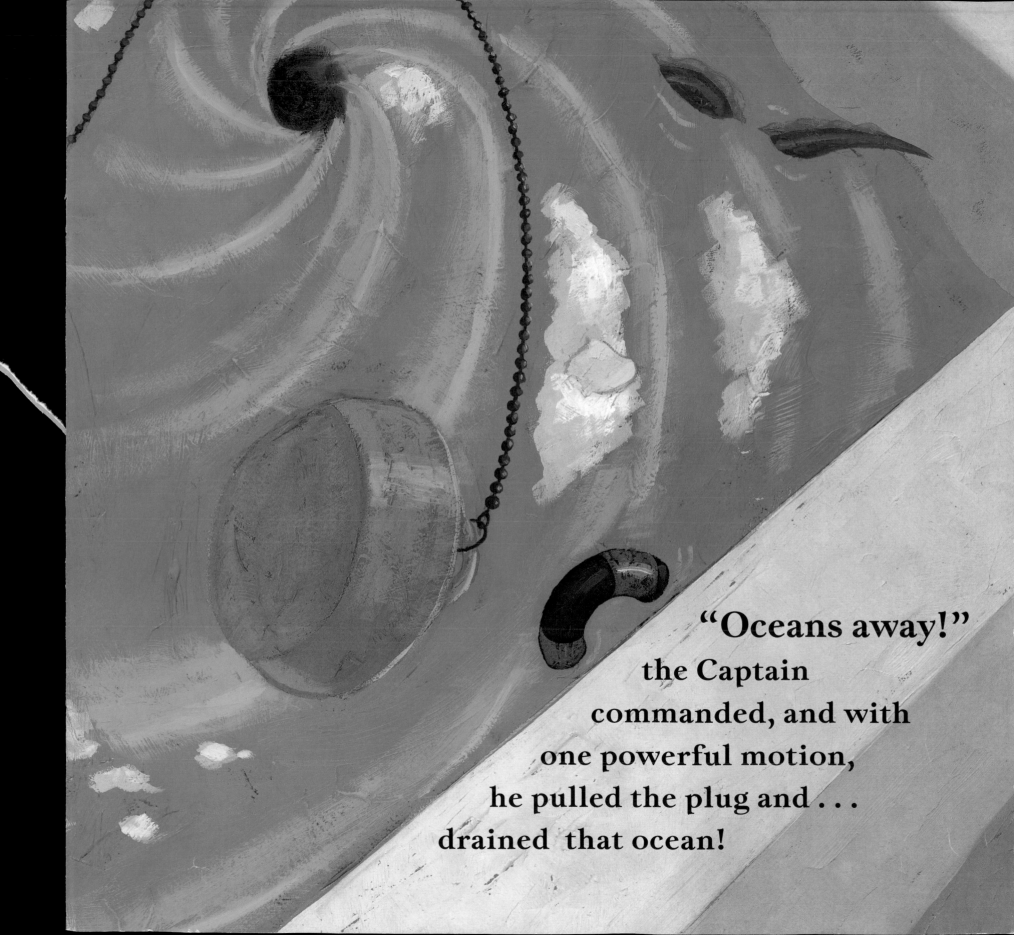

"Oceans away!"
the Captain
commanded, and with
one powerful motion,
he pulled the plug and . . .
drained that ocean!

Down he climbed,
onto dry land, into the
Great Soft Toweling,
leaving his footprints
on the shaggy shore.

There, he was powdered and pajamaed,
combed and brushed, and
covered with kisses.

And why? Because he was Captain Bob,
the bravest and best Captain
that ever sailed the Soapy Seas.
Aye! Aye!

For the Department of Illustration, Cal State Long Beach. —J. C.

For Captain Chris DeMello, with love. —R. S.

Atheneum Books for Young Readers An imprint of Simon & Schuster Children's Publishing Division 1230 Avenue of the Americas New York, New York 10020 Text copyright © 2000 by Roni Schotter Illustrations copyright © 2000 by Joe Cepeda All rights reserved including the right of reproduction in whole or in part in any form. Book design by Michael Nelson The text of this book is set in Lomba Bold. The illustrations are rendered in oil paint. Printed in Hong Kong. 2 4 6 8 10 9 7 5 3 1 Library of Congress Cataloging-in-Publication Data Schotter, Roni. Captain Bob sets sail / written by Roni Schotter; illustrated by Joe Cepeda.—1st ed. p. cm. "An Anne Schwartz book." Summary: Bathtime becomes an adventure as Captain Bob sets out to brave Bath Bay and Faucet Falls. ISBN 0-689-82081-X [1. Baths—Fiction.] I. Cepeda, Joe, ill. II. Title. PZ7.S3765Can 2000 [E]—dc21 98-47071

FIRST EDITION